♡ Baxter is Missing ♡

Read more
OWL DIARIES
books!

OWL DIARIES
♥ Eva's Treetop Festival ♥
1

OWL DIARIES
♥ Eva Sees a Ghost ♥
2

OWL DIARIES
♥ Eva and the New Owl ♥
4

OWL DIARIES
♥ A Woodland Wedding ♥
3

OWL DIARIES
♥ Baxter Is Missing ♥
6

OWL DIARIES
♥ Warm Hearts Day ♥
5

OWL DIARIES
♥ The Wildwood Bakery ♥
7

OWL DIARIES

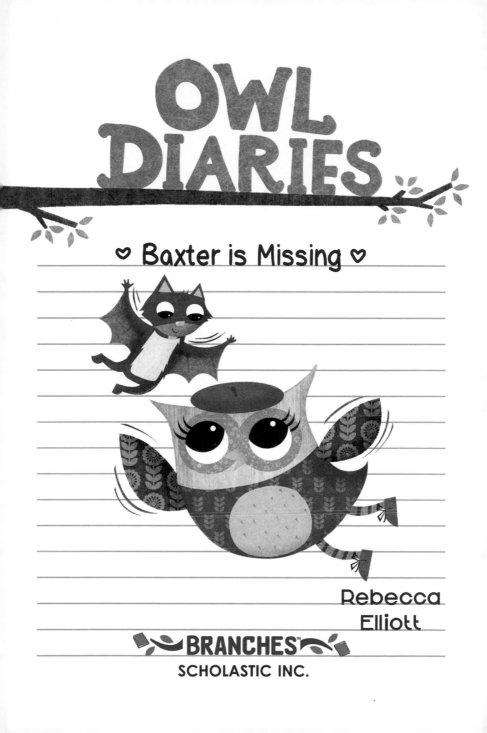

♡ Baxter is Missing ♡

Rebecca Elliott

BRANCHES

SCHOLASTIC INC.

For Mum and Dad, who always find me
when I'm lost. — R.E.

Special thanks to Eva Montgomery.

Library of Congress Cataloging-in-Publication Data

Names: Elliott, Rebecca, author. | Elliott, Rebecca. Owl diaries; 6.
Title: Baxter is missing / Rebecca Elliott.
Description: First edition. | New York, NY: Branches/Scholastic Inc., 2017.
| Series: Owl diaries; 6 | Summary: A famous author is coming to visit
and Eva and her classmates are assigned to write a story — but Eva Wingdale
is totally distracted because her pet bat, Baxter, has gone missing, and
she suspects that the sneaky squirrels
have something to do with her missing pet.
Identifiers: LCCN 2016045591 | ISBN 9781338042849 (pbk.)
Subjects: LCSH: Owls — Juvenile fiction. | Bats — Juvenile fiction. |
Squirrels — Juvenile fiction. | Pets — Juvenile fiction. | Diaries — Juvenile
fiction. | CYAC: Owls — Fiction. | Bats — Fiction. | Squirrels — Fiction. |
Pets — Fiction. | Lost and found possessions — Fiction. | Diaries — Fiction.
Classification: LCC PZ7.E45812 Bax 2017 | DDC [Fic] — dc23 LC record
available at https://lccn.loc.gov/2016045591

ISBN 978-1-338-04285-6 (hardcover) / 978-1-338-04284-9 (paperback)

10 9 8 7 6 5 4 3 2 1   17 18 19 20 21

Printed in China   38
First edition, May 2017

Book design by Marissa Asuncion
Edited by Katie Carella

♥ Table of Contents ♥

♡ We Meet Again! ♡

Sunday

Hello Diary,
  It's me – Eva Wingdale! I still live in
Treetopolis. I'm still super busy. And I
still love lots of different things . . .

I love:

My new paint set

Taking Baxter
for a fly

My teacher

Baking cookies

The word <u>balloon</u>

Starting
new clubs

Reading Owl Ninja books

Writing to friends

I DO NOT love:

My brother's pet
spider Malcolm

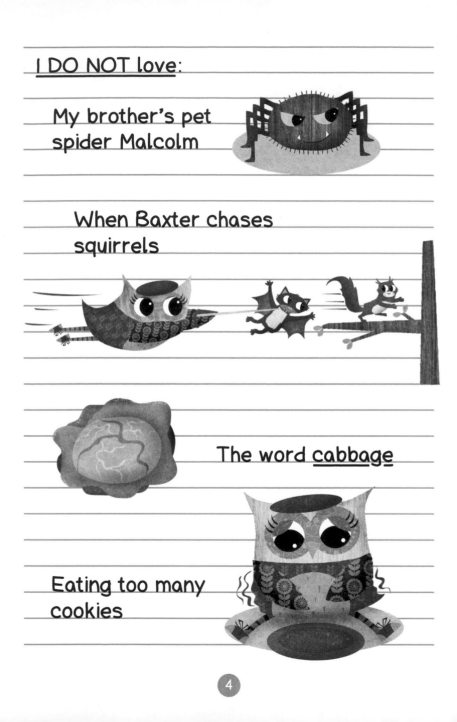

When Baxter chases
squirrels

The word <u>cabbage</u>

Eating too many
cookies

Going to bed when it's still night

Dad's dance moves

Making my bed

Losing things

My family is **OWLSOME**!

Here we are having a picnic:

Dad

Me

Mom

Humphrey

Baby Mo

Here I am with Baxter, my cute little pet bat!

Being an owl is **OWLSOME**, too!

We sleep in the daytime.

We are awake in the nighttime!

A group of us is called a <u>parliament</u>.

And we can fly really fast!

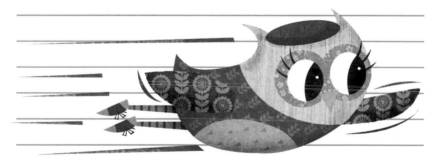

ZOOM!

I live on Woodpine Avenue. My tree house is number 11. Lucy Beakman lives at number 9.

We're best friends – and so are our pets. Here they are dressed in their space suits:

Baxter

Rex

Lucy and I are in Mrs. Featherbottom's class. Here is our class photo:

Macy

Lilly Zara Jacob Carlos

Kiera

Zac

George Lucy Mrs. Featherbottom

Sue

Me

Hailey

Speaking of school, I can't wait to see all my friends tomorrow! I'm off to bed!

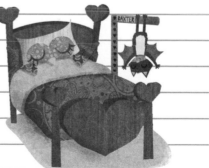

♡The Story Makers Club ♡

Monday

At school Mrs. Featherbottom told us about a **FLAP-TASTIC** class contest.

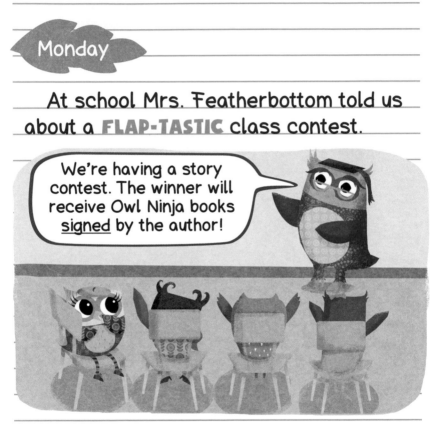

We're having a story contest. The winner will receive Owl Ninja books <u>signed</u> by the author!

Everyone loves the Owl Ninja books! We were all so excited!

Some classmates came up with story ideas right away.

Zara is writing about the Old Oak Tree using her photographs.

Carlos is creating a superhero comic strip called Captain Owlsome.

Sue is writing about herself.

And I . . . could not think of anything to write about.

When in doubt, start a club!

After school we flew to my house. I pulled out my new paint set, and we all painted pictures.

Then we had a paint fight! It was so much fun!

. . . Until Mom came in.

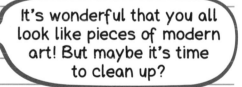

It's wonderful that you all look like pieces of modern art! But maybe it's time to clean up?

Later, I took Baxter for a fly. I was brainstorming story ideas when he pulled me toward the Old Oak Tree.

He probably smelled a squirrel. He's always chasing them, and he loves it when they chase him.

I led Baxter back home.

I worked on my story ideas. But they were all totally terrible! Argh! Maybe I need a good day's sleep . . .

But it is hot! So I'll just open my window first.

That's better.

Good day, Diary.

♡Where is Baxter?♡

Tuesday

Oh Diary! Something awful has happened!
I woke up and Baxter was GONE!

I looked everywhere for him . . .

But he wasn't ANYWHERE!

Then I saw my open window. He must have flown out when I was asleep!

I never should have opened it. This is all my fault!

Mom made **BUGBERRY MUFFINS** for breakfast — my favorite! But I couldn't eat anything.

Sometimes Humphrey is such a squirrel-head.

I couldn't believe I had to go to school at a time like this. But class was actually cool today.

We'll be acting out well-known stories – to help you come up with your own. So everyone, please choose a partner.

We all acted out famous scenes from movies and books.

Star Wings

Owlio and Juliet

Harry Hooter and the Nest of Secrets

Peter Wingspan and Captain Hoot

Snowy White and the Seven Owlets

Hooty and the Beast

It was fun. But I was still worried about Baxter.

We looked for Baxter after school. Rex even tried to sniff him out. But then he just started chasing a squirrel. What is it with pets and squirrels?

Soon, we had to head home.

Oh, Baxter, my lovely bat. Where are you?

♡The Baxter Bunch♡

Wednesday

When I woke up, there was still no sign of Baxter.

Before school, Lucy came over to make "Missing" posters.

We put them up around the forest.

We needed to get to class, so we didn't have time to chase the squirrel.

I knew I needed a plan to find Baxter. So I told everyone what had happened, and I started a new club.

After lunch, Mrs. Featherbottom surprised me.

Eva, I heard that your pet bat is missing. Because we all want to help, our class is going to make Missing Baxter T-shirts today.

Thank you! T-shirts will help spread the word!

We made FLAPERRIFIC t-shirts. (Baxter would love them.)

FIND BAXTER

MISSING

WHERE IS BAXTER?

It was so sweet of everyone to help out!

The Baxter Bunch met after school.

I gave different owls different jobs.

Kiera, Carlos, Jacob, Lilly, and Zara knocked on doors and handed out pictures of Baxter.

Macy, Sue, and Zac put up more Missing posters.

But, Diary, it looks like the posters we hung earlier were taken down! Those stinky squirrels!!

George and Hailey were on squirrel duty, trying to stop them from stealing more posters.

Lucy and I flew around looking for clues. But we didn't find anything.

I feel better knowing that everyone is helping me look for my little Baxter. I just hope he comes home tomorrow.

5

♡The Old Oak Tree♡

Thursday

Everyone worked on their stories at school tonight. But I couldn't think about anything except Baxter.

Eva, why don't you <u>write</u> about Baxter? It might make you feel better.

Good idea, Lucy. I'll give it a try.

So I wrote about . . .

all the costumes Baxter liked to dress up in . . .

the day he learned to fly and smashed into a tree . . .

the time he hid one of Dad's slippers in the toilet . . .

the day I taught him how to jump through a hoop . . .

and the cute face he makes when he wants a cuddle.

It felt good to write about Baxter. But it also made me feel sad.

The Baxter Bunch met at recess.

When was the last time you saw Baxter?

Tell us everything that happened that day.

I tried to remember <u>everything</u>.

I took him for a walk on Monday. He kept trying to fly toward the Old Oak Tree. I think he was chasing a squirrel. Then we flew home. I got ready for bed. Then I opened my window because it was hot. I went to sleep and in the morning . . . Well, he was gone.

When we got to the Old Oak Tree after school, I hoped we would hear the same squeaking noise George heard. But it was raining really hard!

We searched and searched. Then . . .

I flew over to Lilly. She'd found something! She handed it to me.

We searched until we were all wet and cold.

Finally, we went back to my tree house for some hot acorn syrup. It warmed us up right away!

I hoped Baxter was somewhere dry and warm, too.

After everyone went home, Mom came into my room.

It's lovely that your friends are helping you find Baxter, dear.

I know, Mom, but I'm more worried than ever now. Baxter would <u>never</u> take off his collar. He must be in danger.

♡ Stinky Squirrels! ♡

As soon as I got to school, Zara flew over to me. She did not look happy.

I checked those photos I took of the Old Oak tree, but I can't see Baxter in them. I guess I was too far away. Sorry, Eva.

That's okay. Thanks for trying.

Then we had a science lesson. We used magnifying glasses to look really closely at leaves, rocks, and bugs.

Suddenly, Zara HOOTED. Everyone turned to look.

I just used the magnifying glass to look at my photos. And Eva — look!

There he was! Really tiny at the back of Zara's photo.

I knew it! Those stinky squirrels did have something to do with Baxter going missing! I was super angry. And I couldn't stop talking about it all day.

As we were leaving school, Zac spoke up first.

I couldn't believe what Lucy said next . . .

I felt bad for yelling. I was just SO worried about Baxter!

I kept talking about the squirrels during dinner. Then, as I was going to sleep, Humphrey bashed through the door.

Hey, it's true what your friends said. Squirrels can be cool.

But they smell and they steal our food.

You say the same thing about me! Anyway, they don't <u>all</u> smell. And they only steal food when they're hungry.

Hmm. Okay, if you say so, Stinkums.

Hey, watch it, Smelly. Sleep well.

Diary, I'm still SURE the squirrels have done something to Baxter. What if they led him off into the woods and he got lost? Why else would he <u>still</u> be missing?

♡ Baxter the Hero ♡

Saturday

I woke up feeling really bad that I had been so pushy with my friends about the squirrels. I thought that was the end of the Baxter Bunch. But then Lucy showed up, ready to look for Baxter!

Thanks for coming! So sorry about yesterday.

Don't worry, Eva, we all understand what a hard time this is for you.

We made a list of everything we know so we can find Baxter:

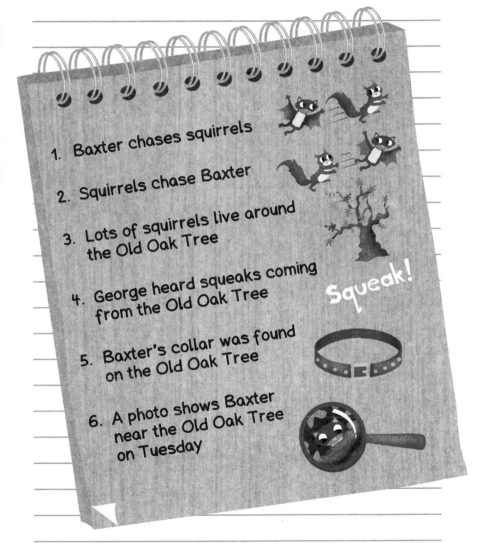

1. Baxter chases squirrels

2. Squirrels chase Baxter

3. Lots of squirrels live around the Old Oak Tree

4. George heard squeaks coming from the Old Oak Tree

Squeak!

5. Baxter's collar was found on the Old Oak Tree

6. A photo shows Baxter near the Old Oak Tree on Tuesday

The squirrels were
squeezing posters
(and everything they
could find!) into a
little hole in the
tree trunk.

MISSING

I darted over to the hole. The squirrels looked so sad. I'd never seen them look like that before. Then I peeked in the tree trunk and saw . . .

He was there! Right down the bottom of a hole! And he was holding a tiny baby squirrel in his arms!

We took off our Baxter T-shirts and put them into the hole. Baxter started to climb up the pile of shirts, with the baby squirrel in his arms.

I remembered Baxter's best trick! I flew down to the ground, grabbed some twigs, and quickly twisted them into a hoop.

Baxter jumped right up out of the hole, through the hoop, and into my arms!

I was so happy to have Baxter back!

The squirrel family looked happy
to have their baby back, too.

(I have to admit it, they looked
pretty cute!)

Back at home,
I gave Baxter his
favorite meal.

Then I read
him his favorite
story.

It's so **WING-CREDIBLE** to have him
home!

Oh, and Diary, I was <u>SO</u> wrong about squirrels! I'll never call anyone a squirrel-head again. (Or only if they've done something really sweet!)

Now I need to find a way to thank everyone who helped me find Baxter.

I know! I'll throw a thank-you party tomorrow!

♡ Let's Party! ♡

Sunday

Hi Diary,
    We partied all day long! Do you want to know where? At the Old Oak Tree, of course!

THE HOOTLES

Everyone who helped Baxter came
to the party. Even Humphrey's band!
It was such a **HOOT**!

I flew home with Baxter after the party. Lucy, George, and Hailey flew with us.

I can't wait for school tomorrow. I've written a great story for the contest.

Me too! I came up with a cool idea after our Story Makers Club paint fight!

How's your story coming along, Eva?

ARRRRRGH!

I TOTALLY FORGOT ABOUT THE
STORY CONTEST <u>TOMORROW</u>!!!

But suddenly,
I had the BEST
story idea EVER!
I stayed up
writing until the
sun was high
in the sky.

♡ A Special Visitor ♡

Monday

Hi Diary,
   Something **OWLMAZING** happened at school today!

We have a special guest today! Everyone, please give a warm welcome to Rebecca Owliott, the author of the Owl Ninja books!

I'm so excited to be here and I can't wait to hear your stories!

I couldn't believe it — the actual author of the Owl Ninja books was HERE in our ACTUAL classroom!

We shared our stories. They were **WING-TASTIC**!

George's story was about a dragon who befriends an owl.

Macy's story was about an owl who goes to the big city.

Hailey's story was about a magic paintbrush.

Sue's story was about "Princess Sue."

And Carlos's comic-strip story was about Captain Owlsome!

But Zara's photo-story was my favorite. It was beautiful and funny!

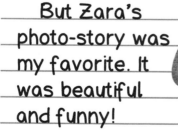

Then it was my turn to share.

You're up, Eva. I believe you have a special guest, too?

That's right!

My story is all about Baxter, the best pet in the world . . .

After I finished my story, Rebecca Owliott flew to the front of the room.

I loved hearing your stories! There are so many flap-tastic writers in this class! It was hard to choose, but . . . the winner is . . .

ZARA!

I was so happy for Zara. She deserved to win! (And she said she'd share the books with the class!) I wanted to win but, really, the best prize is having Baxter back!

Then Rebecca Owliott said we could ask her questions. I put my wing up.

I thought really hard before I answered . . .

I like to write about things I know and about what makes me happy, too. Like my friends and my family. But I also like to write about things I thought I knew but got wrong. Like squirrels. It turns out they're pretty cool.

Luckily, I have Baxter to teach me this. He's pretty smart. He's also great to write stories about! I love you, Baxter.

See you soon, Diary!